P9-EEU-788

Stage Dreams

Melanie Gillman

Graphic Universe™ • Minneapolis

Graphic Universe™
An imprint of Lerner Publishing Group, Inc.
241 First Avenue North
Minneapolis, MN 55401 USA

For reading levels and more information, look up this title at www.lernerbooks.com.

Image credit: The Granger Collection, New York, p. 92.

Library of Congress Cataloging-in-Publication Data

Names: Gillman, Melanie, author, illustrator.
Title: Stage dreams / Melanie Gillman.
Description: Minneapolis : Graphic Universe, [2019] | Summary: In 1861, Grace, a runaway, and Flor, a stagecoach robber, join forces to thwart a plan by the Confederate Army in the New Mexico Territory.
Identifiers: LCCN 2018052140 (print) | LCCN 2018056240 (ebook) | ISBN 9781541561113 (eb pdf) | ISBN 9781512440003 (lb : alk. paper) | ISBN 9781541572843 (pb : alk. paper)
Subjects: LCSH: Graphic novels. | CYAC: Graphic novels. | Robbers and outlaws—Fiction. | Runaways—Fiction. | Transgender people—Fiction. | Confederate States of America—Army—Fiction. | New Mexico—History—1848—Fiction.
Classification: LCC PZ7.7.G543 (ebook) | LCC PZ7.7.G543 St 2019 (print) | DDC 741.5/973—dc23

LC record available at https://lccn.loc.gov/2018052140

Manufactured in the United States of America
1-42258-26121-2/11/2019

To our queer and trans ancestors. Far too many of your stories were lost, but we remember you.

MAP OF NEW MEXICO TERRITORY 1861

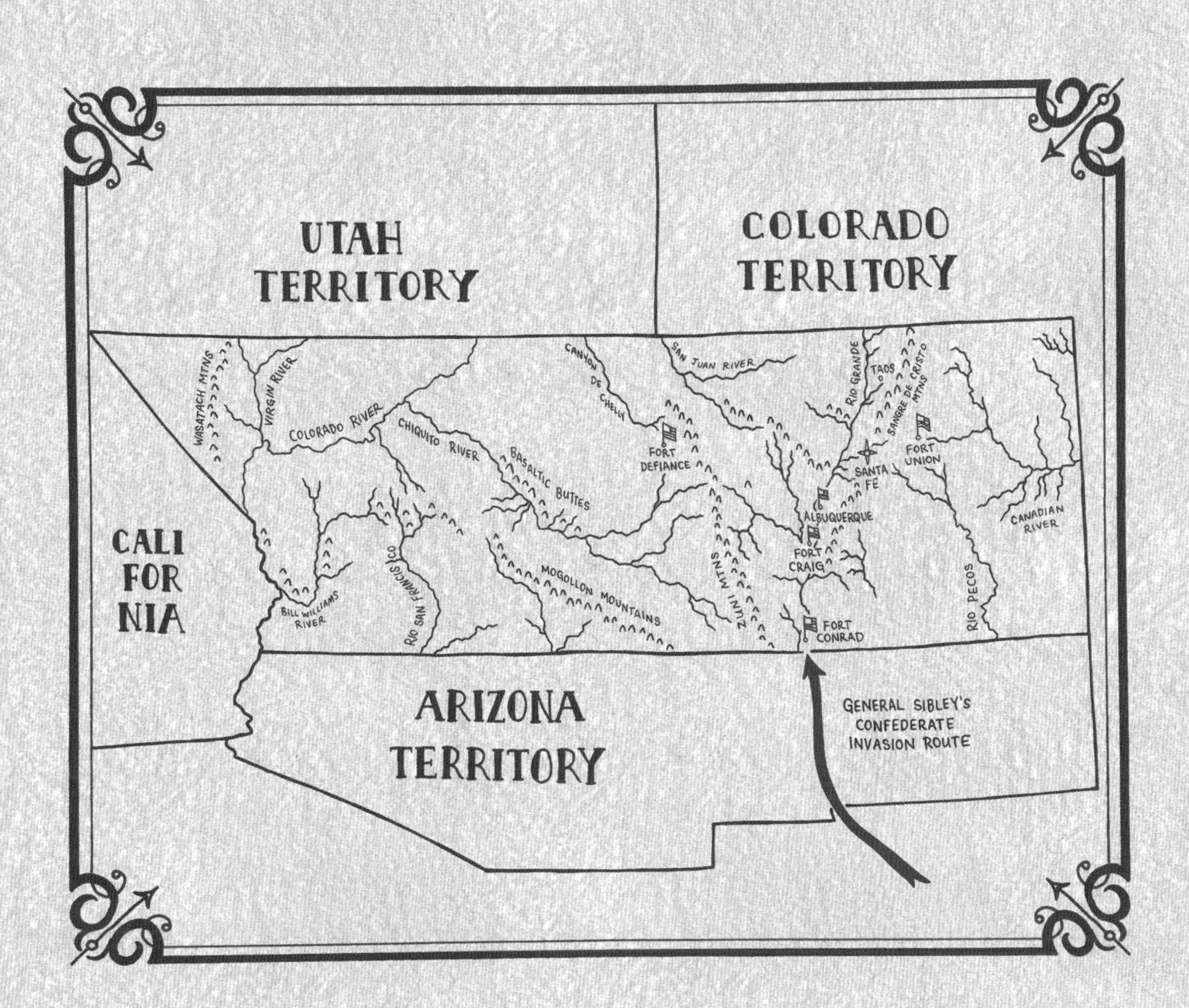
UTAH TERRITORY
COLORADO TERRITORY
CALIFORNIA
ARIZONA TERRITORY
WASATCH MTNS
VIRGIN RIVER
COLORADO RIVER
CHIQUITO RIVER
BASALTIC BUTTES
CANYON DE CHELLY
FORT DEFIANCE
SAN JUAN RIVER
RIO GRANDE
TAOS
SANGRE DE CRISTO MTNS
FORT UNION
SANTA FE
ALBUQUERQUE
CANADIAN RIVER
FORT CRAIG
ZUNI MTNS
MOGOLLON MOUNTAINS
RIO SAN FRANCISCO
BILL WILLIAMS RIVER
FORT CONRAD
RIO PECOS
GENERAL SIBLEY'S CONFEDERATE INVASION ROUTE

CHAPTER
ONE

NEW MEXICO TERRITORY, 1861
Ma'am.
OVERLAND STATION
This yer first time travelin' by coach, miss?

Just sayin'— not every day you see classy ladies like yourself travelin' sans escort out in these parts.

Hmm.
Not much a talker, this one.

That's fine. Just tryin' to be *civil* is all.

What about you, boy? Where you skulkin' off to?

I'm going to Arizona, to enlist under General Sibley!
pft

There's the Confederacy's grand plan for ya, then. Takin' over all New Mexico Territory with an army of *whelps.*
I'm s— eighteen!!
Pounds, maybe.

Leave the boy be.
It's a noble thing at any age— fighting for the liberation of one's homeland.

Sorry— liberation for *who,* again?

Everyone knows General Sibley'll only need a couple weeks to take New Mexico Territory, tops!!
Those Yanks in Arizona rolled over without a fight as soon as his Texans showed up—

Siddown, boy—
he's seized all the guns 'n'artillery from the Union forts, it's gonna be over lickety-split!
'Cept for the Apach givin' him hell fro here to El Paso—
GONNA B ANY DAY NOW!

Never mind all that.
If the Rebs make it all the way up here, they're gonna find themselves up against something *way* worse!

Y'all heard about the GHOST HAWK?

Superstitious *nonsense*.
Ha! Oh ye of little faith–

My brother Wyatt saw it with his *own two eyes* on a mail run outta Prescott, not two months back.

He told me ...
She's a DEMON.
Half woman, half hawk, and mean as SPIT.
She hides in high canyon walls, bidin' her time til a big, fat stage rolls round.
Then she swoops down and carries off the whole damn kit in her talons- people and all!
And flies 'em back to her nest and feeds 'em to her young- ALIVE!

Reckon my brother's the only soul in the whole territory who can say he's looked the Ghost Hawk in the eye...
...and lived to tell about it!

You don't reckon—?
Don't you listen to that bull.

Been driving this route near ten years now. Never seen no "Ghost Hawk."

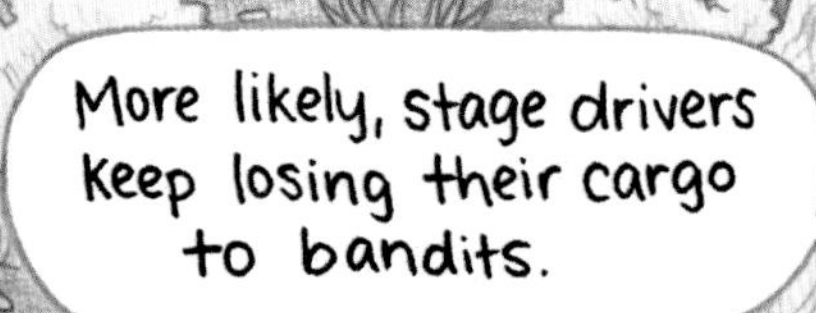
More likely, stage drivers keep losing their cargo to bandits.
Figurin', if they blame it on a monster, maybe they won't lose their job.

And if any ghouls *do* show, well-
-that's what the Remington's for.
!!!

THUNK

The strongbox.
NOW.

OVER LAND
& CO

wAAAGH
PLAM

God's *garters,* is that it??
OVERLAND & CO

I swear, these banks get stingier by the *week.*

FWEEEE

Here ya go!
And don't you *dare* drop it this time.
OVERLAND & CO

S'pose I'll see what goods they got in the cab too.

Do you see anything...?

HOWDY, folks!

Hmm...
P-please don't hurt us, ma'am—

Don't anyone here got anything of value— swear on my life!!

Aww, don't be so hard on yourselves!
I bet *this one's* plenty valuable!

Fine young ladies always make for the best ransoms-

And company!

FWEEEE

CHAPTER
TWO

Welcome home, miss!

I 'spect it ain't as comfortable as what you're used to, but-
Despite appearances, it ain't my intent to hurt you.

Provided you behave yourself.

You sure are a shy one.

Never understood the way you rich ladies go round pretending you're all quiet and demure by nature.
Don't you just wanna punch someone sometimes?
p-please... don't!

—oh

I suspect there's quite a LOT you don't understand about "fine ladies"!

I know how this must look, but please— I can explain—
No need.

What's your name, girl?

My...
my name?

Grace.
My name is Grace.

Pleasure to make your acquaintance, Grace. I'm Flor.
Just pretend I trusted you enough to untie your hands for a sec.

Charmed, I'm sure.
Now then...

What are you on the run from?

Family?
Creditors?
Merciless hand o' the law?

...marriage?

Try *conscription.*

Oh.
Yeah, that'll do it.

The Second Battalion, Georgia Infantry, in fact.
My father signed both of us up as soon as the enlistment call went out.

We're not supporters- Pa has been calling it "rich man's war, poor man's fight."

But we're sharecroppers, and the army promises privates $11 a month-
I'm sure in Pa's mind, that's a new roof for the winter.
Or shoes for the little ones.

Soooo... you're NOT a filthy rich runaway debutante, then.

That *does* throw a wrench in my plan to ransom you...
Sorry to disappoint.

In any case, I couldn't join the army.
For... several reasons.

So I stole some money— and a dress off a line.

I thought if I could just make it as far as California...
What's in California?

Well, it's about the farthest place from Georgia, for one...

But there's also— the STAGE.

The theater in San Francisco is among the finest in the whole country.
Actors travel there from all over the world!

I'm sure it sounds mad, but I've always dreamed of acting, ever since I was a child.

I thought-
maybe if I went somewhere no one knew me-

...maybe...

I've got a real whopper of a dream, myself!
Want some beans?

ONE LAST BIG HEIST!
Enough to put a couple state lines between myself 'n' some pesky warrants, ifyaknowwhatImean

I'll get me a big, green plot o' land, buy a herd of goats, and live out the rest of my days right *honest*.
(With a healthy stash of gold in the cellar, of course.)

...goats?
Only livestock that's useful AND smart.

I *was* planning on bustin' up this big, fancy cotillion in Santa Fe tomorrow.

Rumor has it, the town's been quietly filling up with Southern rail barons all week.
A whole *mess* of 'em will be meeting there in secret.

Everybody knows the Confederates are eyein' the territories up here—
—but there ain't much out in the desert that can help the war effort.
...is that supposed to be a map?
AS I WAS SAYING...

California, though...
California's got gold, lumber, ports, and poor saps who might be roped into enlisting.

If only there were a quick, reliable way to transport all those goods back South!

Those poor boys up at Fort Union have been *very* nervous since the Rebs took Arizona.

So I figured they might be *keenly* interested to hear what a bunch of Southern rail barons talk about when they think no one's listening.

But I can't risk a Confederate runaway telling anyone about the plan—
—So if I can't ransom you, to your folks, I might see what the fort'll give for ya.

No!! Please...

I could...

I- I could help you!
Help you sneak into the cotillion!

I've no love for the Confederacy— there's no way I'd be *here* if I did! But I *know* Confederates.
If you take me with you, I can help talk your way in!

Could you, now?
I told you!
I'm an ACTRESS.

I could pass myself off as a debutante— or a visiting heiress!
I've seen them enough to know how they act.
Done this plenty of times before, then, have ya?

Well... I haven't exactly tested it out on an audience...

...so you'd be the first to hear...

Well, I'm *all* ears.
FINE.
Just give me a minute.

Lands, is that Mr. Johnson over by the punch?
Why, I never—

As I recall, Mr. Johnson last dared show his face at the Brittons' spring garden party—
—hanging about poor dear Miss Lizzie Beaumont all night, like a stricken puppy.

Everyone *knew* he wasn't really after Lizzie— the sweet girl being a bit more good breeding than good sense

Of course, when *Mister* Beaumont heard—
OKAY, OKAY.
I see what you're drivin' at.

Where I come from, folks can pick out the county you were born in and the size of your daddy's pocketbook based on *accent alone*.

Like it or not—
my voice might be the thing that gets you through the door.

And if it works—then I gotta promise not to turn you in, I suppose?

That, and we split the profits fifty-fifty—
SPLIT?!

I have much less incentive to betray you if given a fair stake in the venture.
It's simply good business sense.

W-
what...
What are you...

You *do* got the voice for it.
And you're certainly pretty enough to pull it off.

What? Something I said?

N-no one's ever called me *pretty* before.

KOFF

WELP, time to go water the horse!
Long day ahead tomorrow!

Yup, can't have no THIRSTY HORSES just a-wanderin' round...

HEY!!
Isn't this FIRE a little close to this TREE??
Just holler if it catches, okay!

ughhh.

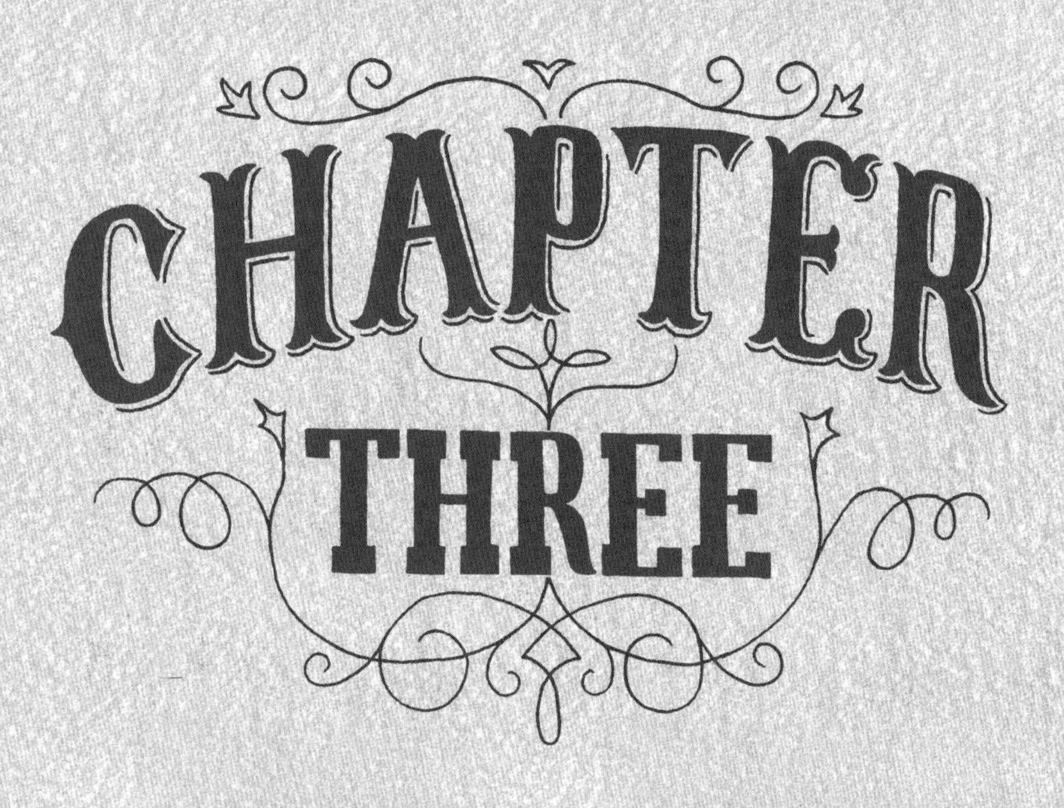
CHAPTER
THREE

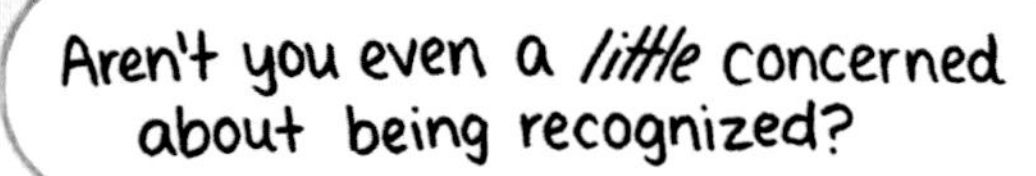
Aren't you even a *little* concerned about being recognized?

Ain't been a problem yet!
Yes, but—

Y'know, once, in a saloon, I ran into a man the Ghost Hawk had robbed the week before.
Y'know what he did?
Looked right past me, like you'd look past a stump.

Folks are real good at seeing what you tell 'em, y'know?
I'm supposed to be some sorta monster—
So that's what they remember robbing them!

That, or no one wants to admit they got their lily hide handed to them by a short brown lady and a bird!

Here it is!

L.R. APONTE
FINE TAILOR
Best dang tailor in the territory!

Hey Luis! You in?

Can I talk ya into closin' up early today?

Did you *already* manage to tear that gaping hole in the seat of your pants back open?
N-no!

Luis, he's a... real kidder.
It's high time you consigned those rags to the flames! But *noooo*, you simply must save those bank deposits for your damn...

...goats.

You've branched out into kidnapping, Flor?
Ahem, This is my new *business partner*, Grace.

Grace traveled here all the way from Georgia to allow me the honor of escortin' her to a high-class Reb cotillion tonight.
So we're in the market for *gala wear*.
Pleasure to meet you, Mr. Aponte.

Helloooo, what's this?
The skirt's hemmed higher in the front than back? Doesn't it drag that way?

It wouldn't if I had a proper crinolette to hold it up! The new ones from Paris are all flat in the front.
I... didn't have one that fit, or I'd be happy to show you...

Flat in the front!
It always takes so long for news like that to reach the territories...

I'll be the first shop for *miles* in the know!
How 'bout closing up to protect your new trade secret, then?

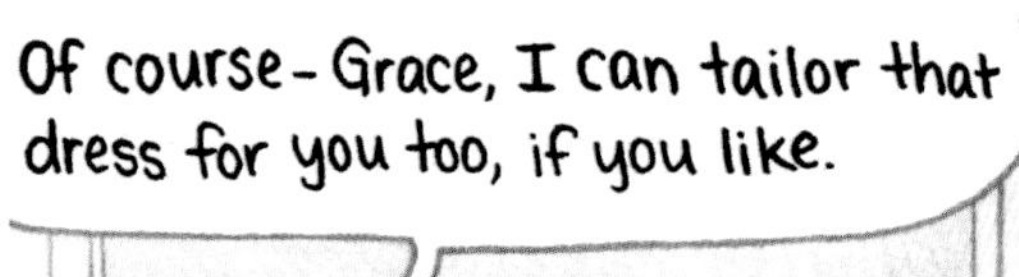
Of course- Grace, I can tailor that dress for you too, if you like.

Crinolette or no, that hem needs letting down!

Is it that obvious?
It wasn't exactly- ah- designed for me.

That's my *specialty*, dear!
Step into my workroom! We'll see if we can find something sufficiently fancy for you.

Now, Grace, I'd love to bend your ear about what else Georgia ladies are wearing this year.
We may be a humble territory, but my customers do like to keep up with the times!
They're all so... tall.

You'd be surprised just how many tall ladies you meet out here.
And it's much easier to shorten a dress than lengthen it!
What do you think?
My mother would kill me – no, *any* of her daughters –
if she caught us with necklines as low as these.

What's gonna look most unsuspicious to a room fulla rich Rebels?

This one, if we can make the bodice sit a little higher...

With a bit less flounce in the front, but more in the back...

And this one, if we double the buttons down the back.

Won't that just make it even *more* an unholy hassle to get on?
The more hassle, the more *expensive* it looks.

Look, this one is even your color!
It brings out—

—the blood of mine enemies!
I was going to say your lips.

I mean... eyes.

Okay, break it up—fitting time!
Ladies first—Flor, you can wait in the next room.

I'm a lady *too*.

You can change behind here, if you'd prefer privacy.
Thank you.

Let me know if those buttons give you any trouble.
Have you put on a gown like this before?

Never this fancy! And only a few times, when I was a kid.
My parents used to indulge me when I was little— letting me play dress-up if I wanted.

They'd even trot me out at dances sometimes.
It—it must've seemed like a silly joke to everyone, back then.

Nobody ever told me to stop. Not in words, at least.
But I knew a day would surely come when I'd walk outside and...
...find the joke had dried up.

I couldn't reach all the buttons by myself, but—
You look lovely.

Your parents, though- they must be worried. Do they know where you are?

No. They don't have any reason to suspect or to come looking for me.

We've never spoken of... well, *anything* like this.
To be honest...
I'd bet they're relieved to be rid of me.

You might be surprised. It's more common than you'd think-
Parents who only want to see their children happy.

Here- make yourself useful.
See if you can unsnarl this for me while I work on your sleeve.

There, move around a bit.
Does everything feel comfortable?

It's a lot lower cut than I'm used to, but—

Mr. Aponte, what do we do if—in spite of everything—we're discovered?

As Union sympathizers?
Well... that too.

Well...
Whatever scheme it is you two have concocted, it's bound to be dangerous.

As I see it, you do have one thing going for you, though.

Neither of you is going in there alone.

The ones who love you-
- they'll protect you.

Oh, no! It's not like that.

I just...
we just...

We're *business partners*.

Well, my mistake.

Actually...
there is one other way you could look at it.

So far, you've only talked about saving your *own* hide. But if you pull this off–
Well, you might do some good. For more than just yourself.
Not everyone who wants a chance like that gets one–
–so it's never to be taken lightly, when opportunities to help *do* come to you.

Well...
goddamn.
Goddamn is right!
Now, let's see about wrestling Flor into that evening gown.

CHAPTER
FOUR

HARDWARE
WANTED
WANTED
WANTED
WANTED
WANTED

I mean it – you *can't* wear that thing into the cotillion.

Excuse you, I have it on good authority rich folks *love* hawks.
They use 'em to hunt –

I dunno, hapless peasants or something.

Not at *galas* they don't!

Besides – one lick of talons and these silk gloves would get torn to shreds!

... and I couldn't bear damaging anything so fine.

Suppose you got a point, though–
Don't want us attracting *too* much attention.
We probably oughta-
WAIT.

Who is *this* gorgeous little lady??

Look at this *face*!!
mweh

You *bet* I have a carrot for you, you little minx...

...if you don't have the *prettiest* eyes...

...bet you got all the neighborhood billies on a string...

Flor... we should probably go.

SIGH
Suppose you're right.

Shall we?
Listen...
You can almost hear the music from here...

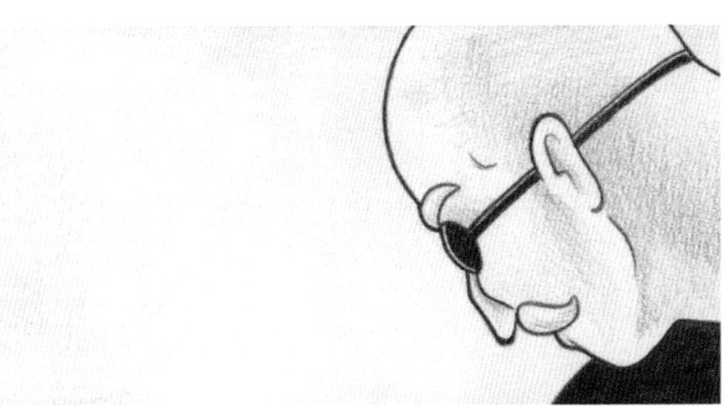

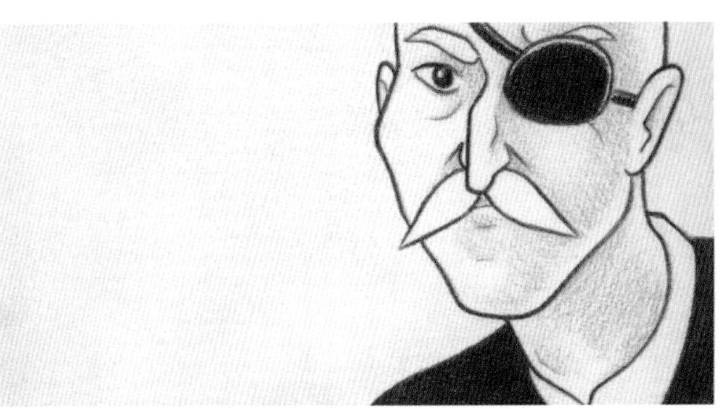

Invitations, ladies?

Invitations?!!
You didn't ask *those* sacks for n

OH, MY!
How very like us to forget!

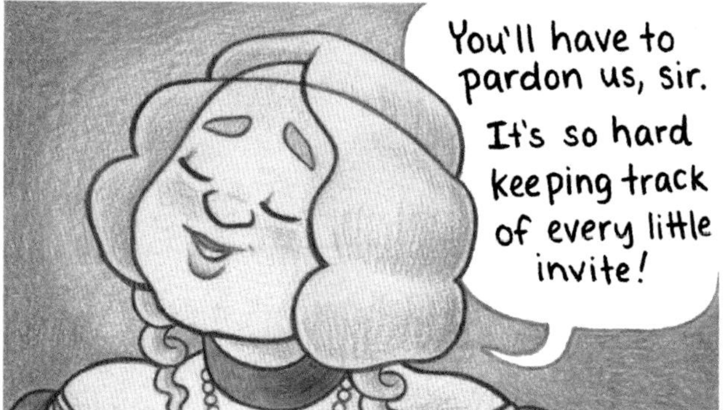
You'll have to pardon us, sir.
It's so hard keeping track of every little invite!

My companion and I are here at the request of my uncle.
He promised to make our introductions, but silly me, I seem to have misplaced him!

Who's this uncle of yours?

I'm happy to bring him out for you, once I find him.
I would hate for you to spend the night worrying after a couple silly girls!

I meant his *name,* girl.

His name—why, Mr. Overland, of course.
Never heard of no Mr. Overland.

I certainly wouldn't expect you to know the name of every gentleman here!
I shall be sure to introduce you when I find him!

Unless you got an invite stuffed down that dress somewhere, you better get looking *outside*—

Morgan, for heaven's sake! Did I hire you to abuse young ladies on my porch?

You must forgive Morgan. He sometimes forgets if he is my doorman or my guard dog.

Oh, no offense taken at all.
One simply *must* keep these events private, after all.

Yeah! Can't have undesirables just *waltzing in* as they please!

... quite.

Come in, my dear—
Let's see if we can hunt down this wayward uncle of yours.

I don't believe we've had the pleasure of meeting before.
I'm Francis Adair. What did you say your name is, child?
Grace Overland, sir.

Forgive me, but you are visiting from Georgia, no? Chatham County, perhaps? Your accent—
Why, you have an impeccable ear, Mr. Adair!

I so rarely get to enjoy the sounds of home this far west. Ladies are always in such short supply—
And true Georgian ladies, practically unheard of!
You poor dear!

Please—may I offer you a drink?

That's very kind of you! But I'd hate to keep you from your other guests...

Nonsense. What sort of host would I be to abandon you?

In fact—here's an idea.

A number of visiting Georgian gents are meeting in the upstairs parlor. Dull business matters, of course—
—but perhaps one is your missing uncle?
That *would* be the spot for him...

Right this way, my dear...

I'd remove that hand if you like it *attached*.

Excuse me-
You must forgive my companion!!
When women travel alone, among so many strange men, we must be overzealous in guarding each other's virtue!
It's true!
One meets so many of a- coarser nature on the road!

You poor dears.
I fear the recent tensions in the territories have only made things more dangerous for our young ladies.
Believe me, for us gentlemen, this has been a topic of much discussion.

When this war is over, we will at last be able to make this land *safe*.

There is *much* work to be done.

CHAPTER
FIVE

They still at it, Frank?
Yes, sir.

Evening, gentlemen.

We have some ladies visiting from Georgia, looking for a Mr. Overland.
Has anyone seen him?
Maybe you, Col. Benoit?

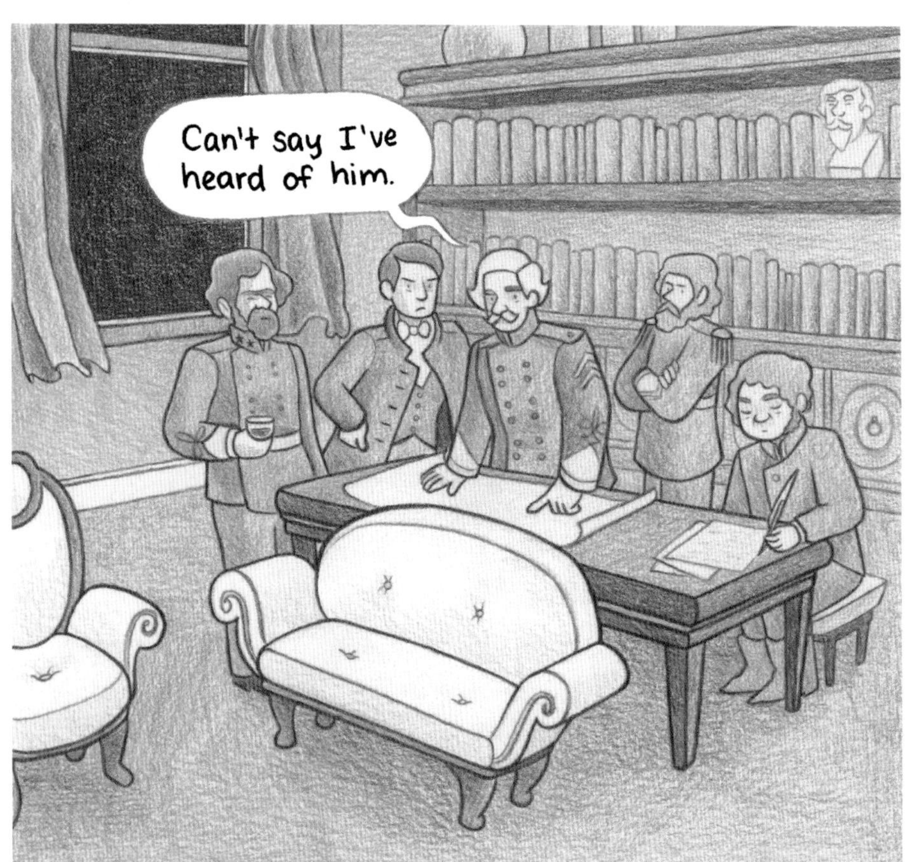
Can't say I've heard of him.

But I'm sure the territori
are full of Overla

I can hardly clai
to know the

Ah, oh well. Paul, would you mind asking around downstairs after Mr. Overland?
Right away, sir.

Please make yourselves comfortable, ladies. I'm sure we'll have him tracked down in no time!

This is a closed meeting, Adair.
Oh, it's just a couple girls!

...and perhaps the presence of ladies will have a *civilizing* effect on you brutes.
ha
ha ha
ha
ha

Seems to be several folks here missing family...

Did Paul ever find that kid of his? The deserter?

Not that I heard - still on the lam.
I tell yo these youn are all cowar

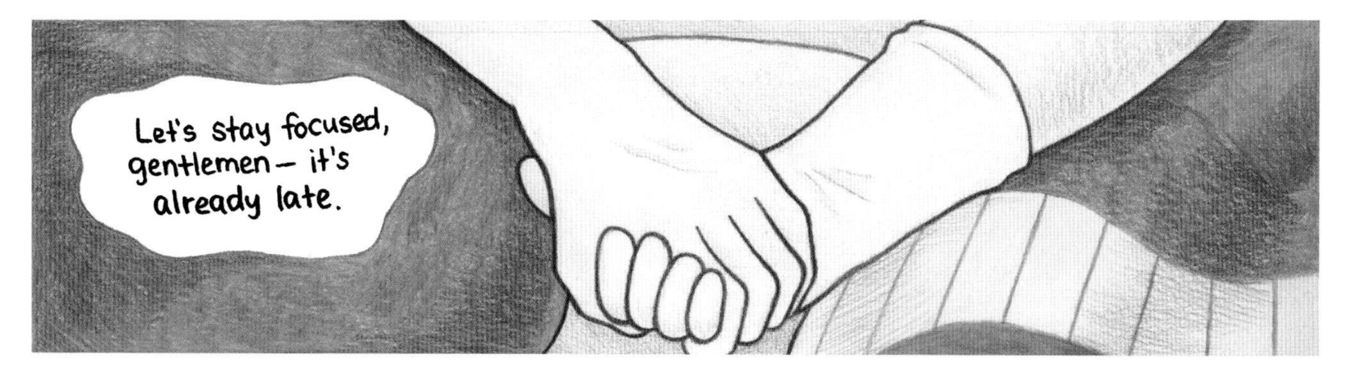
Let's stay focused, gentlemen - it's already late.

Now, we've got landowners in these three counties who are willing to lease quarter-mile strips of their plots for railroad development, to help our cause...
SANTA FE

Hey, Morg–
You let in anybody by the name of Overland?

Nope.
Been lookin', too.

Funny sorta name, "Overland."

Only ever heard of the stagecoach company.

I don't like it.

Something's off.
Just don't know *what* yet.

Well, if you sort it out, let us know, okay?
Lord knows we ain't paid enough for bootlicking *and* trouble.

We've been negotiating with the claims offices here, here, and here along the coast.

Much of this is unexplored territory— the mineral resources should be intact, even after the rush back in '49.

There are natural streams and virgin woodlands here, here, here, and here.

Even if the plots fail to yield gold or silver veins, the lumber may prove just as valuable for the cause.
Um— excuse me—

What are you *doing?*

BAM
BAM
BAM

THE GHOST HAWK
THAT WOMAN IS THE GHOST HAWK!
Gentlemen.
NOBODY MOVE, OR I SLICE THIS GIRL RIGHT OPEN!!

What are you DOING??

A little HELP here??
oh...
OH!

Everybody back, right now!! I'll do it!!
Oh, please! Listen to her!

You!! Funny face!! Open that door!!
p-please...
FLOR!!

FLOR!!

Child-
are you
all right?

I...

Oh *thank* God.

Thank god you're safe.
Get yourself out of here.
Private...

Oh, Colonel, pardon me!
I didn't see you there...
FWEEEE

STOP!!

CHAPTER
SIX

uUUUUUGH

How long was I out?
Shh. Not long.

Well, good news is, the bleeding stopped. You've got one impressive lump, though. How's it feel?
Christ's corset—hell of a throb.

I tell ya what—I'm gonna think twice next time I get the notion to bust a bottle on someone's skull.

Is that... whiskey?
Figured it'd be cleaner than the horse trough.

Ha... probably true.

For your first taste of outlaw life, that didn't go so well, did it.

I can think of several ways it could have gone worse.

... you could've just... left me there.

I didn't.

I just can't believe—
—all that, and we've got *squat* to show for it!

We were *so close!!*
One more minute and I could've snatched that blasted map, and—

Oh— this map?

AAAAAAAAA

AAAAA!!
YOU!!

You incredible girl.
oh... whoops
Haha, no more spinning with *head wounds*, okay??

You're gonna take San Francisco by storm.

Stage Dreams, Annotated

Page 9

In 1861, New Mexico Territory was still part of the Union (the United States of America), at least on paper. New Mexicans were divided about the Civil War—many people supported the Union, many people supported the Confederacy, and many people thought New Mexico should have nothing whatsoever to do with a war happening on the other side of the country. New Mexico was about to get dragged into the war whether it liked it or not, though. In July 1861, Confederate troops managed to take over the southern half of the territory. They renamed it the Confederate Territory of Arizona. Soon after, Confederate brigadier general Henry Hopkins Sibley began making plans to advance into the northern half of the territory, with hopes he could take over Albuquerque, Santa Fe, and the gold mines of Colorado en route to California.

Page 16

The strongbox here is filled with demand notes—the first paper money to achieve wide circulation in the United States. The US Treasury first printed demand notes in August 1861. Prior to the Civil War, US dollars were all coins minted from precious metals such as gold and silver; unlike paper money, the coins had inherent value. Paper money was controversial and unpopular when it first debuted in the United States, because people didn't trust that pieces of paper would keep their value over time! You can imagine how frustrating this would be for an outlaw in 1861, robbing a stagecoach and hoping to find it full of gold, only to end up with a chest full of nothing but paper.

Page 22

Despite how frequently they're erased from history books, we can still find a handful of records of transgender people living in early American history! The total number of surviving pre-twentieth century records is relatively small, but that doesn't mean there weren't many trans people at the time. More likely, few records exist because trans people were forced to live stealthily throughout most of US history. Surviving accounts of historical trans people were usually only written if the person in question was publicly outed—often by law enforcement, medical professionals, or coroners after the person's death.

Mary Jones was a Black trans sex worker who was put on trial in New York in 1836 after she pickpocketed a few of her clients; her trial became a public scandal in part because she was trans. Mrs. Nash, a trans cook and laundress, worked for Lieutenant Colonel George Armstrong Custer's 7th Cavalry just a few years before the Battle of Little Bighorn. She also married three different men in the course of her lifetime. Her trans identity wasn't discovered until after her death.

Hundreds of AFAB (assigned female at birth) people dressed as men to enlist in the army on both sides of the Civil War. While not all of them were trans, there are a few accounts of veterans who continued to live as men for the rest of their lives, including Albert Cashier, a member of the 95th Illinois Infantry Regiment. Other examples of trans men in the American West include Mountain Charley (a one-eyed stagecoach driver and famed crack shot with a pistol) and Harry Allen (an outlaw and a rare example of an out trans man in the nineteeth century). Many Indigenous nations in the West also included two-spirit people, such as We'wha, a famous mediator and member of the Zuni tribe. We'wha lived in New Mexico in the latter half of the nineteeth century. Most likely, there are thousands of other historical trans Americans whose names we will never know, either because their records were lost or erased or because they managed to keep their trans identity a secret throughout their life.

Albert Cashier, a trans man who served in the 95th Illinois Infantry Regiment during the US Civil War.

Page 24

Grace says she wants to avoid "conscription," but the Confederate army didn't officially institute a draft until April 1862. In my mind, Grace is using the word that best describes the sense of entrapment she feels. In the South, community expectations, family obligations, and financial destitution would all be strong forces pushing her to enlist, draft or no draft. Running away was her best option to avoid military service.

Page 25

"Rich man's war, poor man's fight" was a common complaint of low-income people on both sides of the Civil War. In the South, many poor white people viewed the war as something they would be forced to die for but which would only benefit the interests of the land- and slave-owning rich. However, this anti-war stance does not excuse poor white Southerners from racism—even if they were against the war, the vast majority of them were still pro-slavery. I included this detail in the book in part because numerous contemporary writers and historians, in their attempts to romanticize the Confederacy, often gloss it over. Promoting a historical image of Southerners as uniformly eager to fight and die in the war makes it easier to, for instance, defend Confederate monuments or pretend the Confederate flag represents nothing except "Southern heritage."

Page 29

Flor is alluding to a cross-country railroad line here! In 1861, the Union navy was blockading all Confederate ports in the Atlantic—which posed a huge problem for the South, the economy of which relied on trade with Europe. The Confederacy desperately needed gold and ports, so taking over the West and building a transcontinental rail line to the California coast would have given it a huge advantage in the war.

Page 30

Even though it hadn't happened yet, the Union army knew the Confederate army was planning to invade the northern half of New Mexico Territory. Given the relative ease with which Confederate troops overtook Arizona Territory in the summer of 1861, Union outposts in New Mexico were likely more than a little worried about the coming invasion. Flor is right here—this means the Union side would eagerly welcome stolen plans and documents from the Confederate army.

Page 31

Grace and Flor's plan here is far from outlandish—lots of women served as spies, on both sides of the Civil War! Women spies may even have had some advantages over men. Because of sexist stereotypes, men were more likely to view women as naive, innocent, or stupid—and therefore completely incapable of spying. Elizabeth Van Lew, a wealthy Virginia socialite, smuggled military secrets to the Union side (often hidden inside hollowed-out eggs) for the entire length of the war. Mary Bowser, a free Black woman, voluntarily posed as a servant in Jefferson Davis's Confederate White House so she could pass invaluable state secrets along to Union general Ulysses S. Grant. Pinkerton detectives including Kate Warne and Hattie Lawton helped foil an assassination attempt against Abraham Lincoln in 1861. Other famous Civil War women spies include Harriet Tubman, Rose O'Neal Greenhow, Pauline Cushman, Sarah Emma Edmonds, and many more.

Page 42

Although the population of Black people in New Mexico has never been large relative to other states, records show Black people living in this area at least as far back as the seventeenth century, during Spanish colonization. In 1860, the US census shows only a few dozen Black New Mexicans—but those numbers may be misleading. Many New Mexicans likely had a mixture of African, Latinx, Indigenous, or European ancestry by the time of the Civil War; and mixed-race people who could present and register as a non-Black person may have found advantages in doing so.

Page 43

High fashion of the nineteenth century tended to originate in Europe. Trends sometimes took as long as a year to make their way across the Atlantic to the United States—and then even longer to reach the landlocked western territories. Wealthy families on the Atlantic coast would've been the first to wear new English and French fashions. By hearing this insider report from Georgia via Grace, Luis can update his shop's selections and potentially edge out his competitors for a few months.

Page 45

Fun fact: Coat hangers weren't invented until 1869, so I had to come up with a different solution for how Luis would display sample dresses for his customers. Unless a tailor could afford tons of mannequins, wall pegs were probably the way to go.

Page 50

The bird-shaped object on the table is a sewing bird! This metal clamp could be attached to the side of a table, sometimes with a pin cushion on top of it. The bird's beak could open and then "bite" down on a piece of cloth, holding the cloth in place while a person worked on it.

Page 60

The building where the Confederate cotillion takes place is based on the Santa Fe Governor's Mansion, which wasn't built until 1870. I couldn't find any other historic buildings in the area in 1861 that had quite the look I was going for, so I ended up using it anyway! Mea culpa.

Page 66

A bunch of Confederates throwing a big party in the middle of what is technically Union territory is definitely bold but not totally out of the question. Plenty of Confederates and Confederate sympathizers populated New Mexico Territory, so a bunch of rich people having a party "just for friends" (and quietly discussing business in a locked back room) was—while risky—not impossible.

Page 76

The Confederates were really banking on Californian gold to help sustain them through the war, which is one of the reasons they were so eager to take over the western territories and start building rail lines. This, luckily, never quite *panned out* for them.

Page 97

The structure in the background is Fort Union, one of the main Union army strongholds along the Santa Fe Trail. This fort had to be rebuilt several times during the nineteenth century. The version Flor and Grace would have seen in 1861 was a short-lived earthworks structure—a giant mud fort! This fort helped defeat the Confederate invasion of New Mexico in 1862 but was in such a state of disrepair afterward that Union forces soon abandoned it. After the Union victory, a new fort was built in the same area, out of sturdier materials such as brick, stone, and lumber. It lasted until 1891. You can still visit the ruins of that final Fort Union today.

Acknowledgments

I'm indebted to a number of people for their help and support with this book. Thank you to Mey Rude and Sarah W. Searle for their invaluable feedback on early drafts of this story. To Dylan Edwards, for the thankless work he did helping to prepare each page for print, and for patiently listening to me babble about this book so many times. To all the incredible other writing and artist fellows of the Tulsa Artist Fellowship, whose friendship kept me grounded during so many late nights in the studio. To my secret Twitter friends, who I love. To all my Patreon supporters, who made it possible for me to turn down other work to focus on this book. To my amazing agent, Jen Linnan, who has been a tireless advocate for my work. To Greg Hunter, my editor, whose patience and good sense helped make this the best version of this book it could be. And to my family, for supporting me and believing in me even when my dream of making queer comics seemed like a far-fetched one.

About the Author

Melanie Gillman is an award-winning cartoonist and colored pencil artist who draws positive queer and trans comics for young readers. Their webcomic and graphic novel *As the Crow Flies* (Iron Circus Comics) has been named a 2018 Stonewall Honor Book, won the 2018 Excellence in Graphic Literature Award for Best Middle Grade Graphic Novel, and received nominations for an Eisner, Ignatz, and Dwayne McDuffie Award. In addition to their comics work, they are also an adjunct professor in the Comics MFA Program at the California College of the Arts.